Franklin Has a Sleepover

Franklin

Kids Can Press acknowledges the financial support of the Ontario
Arts Council, the Canada Council for the Arts and the Government
of Canada, through the BPIDP, for our publishing activity.

Published in Canada by
Kids Can Press Ltd.
25 Dockside Drive
Toronto, ON M5A 0B5

www.kidscanpress.com

The hardcover edition of this book is smyth sewn casebound.
The paperback edition of this book is limp sewn with a drawn-on cover.
Manufactured in Buji, Shenzhen, China, in 10/2010 by WKT Company

CM 96 0 9 8 7 6 5 4
CDN PA 96 20 19 18 17 16 15 14 13 12 11

Library and Archives Canada Cataloguing in Publication

Bourgeois, Paulette
        Franklin has a sleepover / Paulette Bourgeois, Brenda Clark.

ISBN 978-1-55453-736-5

1. Franklin (Fictitious character : Bourgeois) – Juvenile fiction. I. Clark,
Brenda II. Title.

PS8553.O85477F687 2011   jC813'.54   C2010-906683-9

Kids Can Press is a **lorus** Entertainment company

Franklin Has a Sleepover

Written by Paulette Bourgeois
Illustrated by Brenda Clark

Kids Can Press

FRANKLIN could count by twos and tie his shoes. He could zip zippers and button buttons. He could even sleep alone in his small, dark shell. So Franklin thought he was ready for his first sleepover. He asked his mother if Bear could stay overnight.

"All right," said Franklin's mother. "But where will Bear sleep?"

Franklin's room was small for a turtle *and* a bear.

"We could sleep in the living room," suggested Franklin. "And we could have a campfire outside and ..."

"Wait a minute!" laughed Franklin's mother. "You haven't even asked Bear yet."

Bear did a happy dance after Franklin called.
"May I please go?" he asked.

His parents worried that the two friends would keep each other awake all night.

"We'll sleep," promised Bear.

Then they wondered if he would feel homesick.

"Not me!" said Bear.

So his parents said yes.

Bear called Franklin. "I can come! I can come!" he shouted.

Franklin could hardly wait. Bear wouldn't arrive until after supper, and Franklin had just finished lunch. So he sorted all his toys and picked Bear's favourites. He made sure there was enough to eat. He even tidied his room. Franklin wanted everything to be just right for his first sleepover.

Bear was excited, too. He couldn't decide what to bring and what to leave behind. He filled an enormous bag with toys, books, a pillow, a sleeping bag, a puzzle and a flashlight. He packed slippers, a toothbrush and a snack. He put his bunny on top of the bag. And every hour he asked if it was time to go.

After supper, Franklin sat by the window, waiting for his friend. Finally, Bear and his parents arrived.

"Have a good time," they said. Bear gave them each a great big hug.

"We're camping in the living room," said Franklin.

"Oh, I've never done that before," said Bear.

He laid out his sleeping bag and Franklin made a tent from a tablecloth.

"This is going to be so much fun," giggled Bear.

They played all their favourite games. Before long it was dark outside.

"How about a campfire?" asked Franklin's father.

"With marshmallows?" Bear licked his lips.

"And hot dogs too," said Franklin's mother.

Franklin's father told Bear and Franklin what to do. They gathered sticks and twigs at the edge of the woods and helped to lay the fire. They filled a bucket with sand and another with water.

"I'll light the fire," said Franklin's mother.

There was a crackle, and sparks jumped into the air.

"I went to camp," said Franklin's father. "We used to sing while the fire was burning."

He sang in a clear, low voice. By the end of the song, Franklin and Bear had learned all the words. The frogs in the pond were croaking, and the owl in the woods was hooting.

Franklin and Bear toasted marshmallows and roasted hot dogs. Bear had two of everything. Then for a long, long time they sat quietly, watching the stars.

Franklin yawned and Bear rubbed his eyes.

"Time to put out the fire and go inside," said Franklin's father.

When Franklin and Bear were ready for bed, Franklin's parents gave them both a glass of water and a good-night hug.

"Sleep tight," they said, turning off the light.

The two friends lay still for a moment. Then Bear turned on his flashlight.

"Franklin?" he whispered. "I don't feel good."

"Did you eat too much?" asked Franklin.

"No," sniffed Bear. A tear ran down his cheek.

"What's wrong then?"

Bear looked around. "I miss my room."

"Oh," said Franklin. Then he had an idea.
"Bring your bed and come with me. We can sleep
in my room."

Bear found a cosy spot and snuggled into his sleeping bag. After a moment, he turned on his flashlight again.

"What's wrong now?" Franklin asked.

"My mother always says good night to my bunny," whispered Bear.

So Franklin gave the bunny a hug. "Good night, Bunny. Good night, Bear," he said.

Soon they were fast asleep.

The next morning, Franklin's father made them
a special breakfast.

"Did you have a nice sleepover?" asked
Franklin's mother.

"It was wonderful," said Bear. "Thank you. Next
time, may Franklin come to my house?"

"Of course," Franklin's parents laughed.
Franklin did his own happy dance.
"And, Bear," said Franklin, tapping his shell,
"don't worry about where I will sleep. I always
bring my own cosy bed with me!"